Favorite Tales of
Monsters and Trolls

A Random House PICTUREBACK®

Favorite Tales of

Monsters

and Trolls

Retold by George Jonsen

Illustrated by John O'Brien

Random House · New York

The Three Billy Goats Gruff

Once upon a time there were three billy goats named Gruff who lived together on a mountainside. There was not much to eat in their rocky pasture, but they could see a field of sweet green grass just across a deep valley.

To reach the green pasture the three billy goats had to cross a bridge, and under the bridge lived a fierce troll.

One day the youngest billy goat began to *trip-trop* across the bridge. At once the wicked troll shouted, "Who goes tripping over my bridge?"

"It is only I, the littlest Billy Goat Gruff," answered the goat in a tiny little voice.

"Fine!" said the troll. "I am going to come up and eat you!"

"Oh, no," said the littlest Billy Goat Gruff. "I am much too small to make a good meal for you. Wait for my bigger brother. He will be coming along soon."

The troll grumbled and rumbled, but he finally let the little goat cross the bridge.

Not long afterward the second Billy Goat Gruff came *trip-trop, trip-trop* across the bridge.

"Who goes there?" shouted the troll, and his big head peered over the bridge.

"It is only I, the middle-sized Billy Goat Gruff."

"Aha!" roared the troll. "I am going to eat you up."

"But sir, I am really not so very big," said the middle-sized billy goat. "If you want a good meal, wait for my bigger brother."

The wicked troll grumbled and rumbled, but he finally let the second billy goat cross the bridge.

In just a little while the third Billy Goat Gruff came *trip-trop, trip-trop, trip-trop* onto the bridge.

He was so heavy that
the bridge creaked and groaned.

"Who is that tramping and stamping over my bridge?" roared the troll.

"It is I, the great big Billy Goat Gruff," the third goat roared back.

"Aha! I've been waiting for you," said the troll. "I am going to come up and eat you!"

The wicked old troll, not knowing what was in store for him, scrambled onto the bridge.

But the big Billy Goat Gruff was not afraid. He just lowered his big strong head and . . .

. . . pushed the troll right off the bridge. The monster went flying down, down, down—into the valley below.

Then the great big Billy Goat Gruff joined his two brothers in the green pasture. The grass was delicious and every day the three goats ate to their hearts' content. Never again were they afraid to cross over the bridge.

The Trolls and the Pussy Cat

There was once a hunter in the far north who caught a bear the like of which he had never seen before. This bear was so white and so big and so tame that the hunter decided to give him to the King of Denmark as a Christmas present.

But before the hunter had reached the border, the snow began to fall. The wind howled and ice froze on his face. The hunter decided to stop at a small farmhouse along the road.

He knocked loudly at the door, and it opened at once. There stood
the farmer and his family, all bundled up in heavy coats and boots.

"May I stay the night with you?" asked the hunter. "The snow and
ice have frozen me and my poor bear through and through."

"Ah! You would not want to stay in *this* house," said the farmer.
"Every Christmas Eve a pack of trolls come down from the mountain
to plague us. They eat our food, they sleep in our beds. We are lucky if
they don't break all our dishes and tables and chairs in the bargain."

"As for us," said the farmer's wife, "we plan to spend the night in a
cave in the woods."

"Well," said the hunter, "I think that if you would let me and my bear stay the night with you, you would not have to move to the cave."

So the bear crept under the table, the hunter rolled up in a blanket on the hearth, and the farmer's family went to sleep in their own beds.

But they did not sleep for long. At midnight came a fearful howling outside the door.

"Farmer Neils! Farmer Neils!" called a terrifying voice. "We have come for our Christmas dinner. Open the door and let us in."

The door burst open, and in rushed a pack of the most ugly, fearsome creatures the hunter had ever seen. They opened the cupboards and pulled out the dishes. They broke into the pantry and carried out great heaping platters of food that the farmer's wife had been cooking all week long.

Suddenly one of the smaller trolls caught sight of the bear's white snout poking out from under the table top. "Look here!" he shouted. "I see a pussy cat!...Nice pussy cat." The troll stuck a long stick with a sausage at one end right into the bear's nose.

With a roar, the huge bear lunged out from under the table. He grabbed the pesky troll and threw him right out the door.

Never did anyone see such a scuffling and a flurry! Trolls were scrambling out the door. Trolls were leaping out the windows. One troll even climbed up the chimney.

The next morning the hunter and his bear set off for the Kingdom of Denmark, well nourished with the food that had been prepared for the trolls. And from that day forward no more trolls came to eat Christmas dinner at the farmhouse, for the news about Farmer Neils and his enormous pussy cat soon spread far and wide in troll land.

The Stone Cheese

There was once an old man who lived with his three sons in a small wooden house at the edge of a forest. The nights were growing long and cold, so one morning the old man asked his eldest son to go into the woods and chop down a tree for firewood.

The eldest brother grumbled and groaned for he did not like to work. But finally he went off with the smallest ax in the house.

When he reached the forest, he found the softest, rottenest old tree that he could. He had scarcely taken one whack at it before he felt a tap on his shoulder.

He spun around, and there stood the ugliest, meanest-looking troll anyone could imagine. The monster had one red eye in the center of his forehead and a big nose shaped like an overgrown carrot.

"Hey, you, floppy fingers!" shouted the troll. "You chop down one tree in this forest and I'll break you into two pieces."

Since the eldest brother much preferred to stay in one piece, he threw down his ax and ran toward home as fast as his legs could take him. He told his father he'd never go into the forest again.

The next morning it was the second son's turn to go for firewood. Bragging that no troll was going to frighten him, he took a bigger ax and picked a taller tree.

Scarcely had he begun to chop when the same ugly troll leaped down out of the treetop and landed on his head.

"Hey, you, spindly legs!" shouted the troll. "You chop down one tree in this forest and I'll break you into three equal pieces."

The second brother had no wish to see himself in three pieces, so he threw down his ax and raced home as fast as his legs could take him.

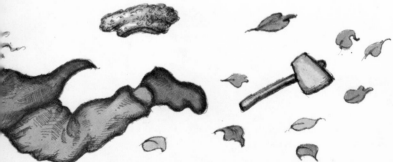

The next day it was the turn of the youngest brother. This brother had more brains than the other two combined. He picked the biggest ax in the house and took a hard, white ball of cheese from the cupboard.

When the older brothers saw him putting the cheese into his bag, they laughed and jeered.

"Are you planning to feed that cheese to the troll?" they asked.

But the youngest brother paid no attention to their sneers.

"Who knows what use I will find for the cheese," he said. And off he went, with his bag swinging along behind him.

When he reached the forest, he picked the tallest tree on the whole mountainside and went to work with his ax. He had scarcely taken three strokes before the troll came running up to him.

"Hey, you, flappy ears!" he shouted. "You chop down one tree in this forest and I'll break you into four pieces."

"You just try it," cried the lad, "and I'll squeeze you into a blob of white jelly just as easily as I squeeze the water out of this stone." Taking the big, white cheese out of his bag, he squeezed it with both hands. Juice squirted out of the cheese—right into the troll's big eye.

"Hey! Hey!" shouted the troll, jumping up and down. "That's enough. I don't want to be crushed like that stone. Just spare me and I'll chop down all the trees you wish. I'll even cut them up into logs and haul them back to your house."

As soon as he heard that, the lad agreed to spare the troll. And from that day on, the ugly monster saw to it that the old man and his sons had all the firewood they needed.